THE QUEEN'S HANDBAG

Steve Antony

To Donald

First published in 2015 by Hodder Children's Books
This paperback edition published in 2016

Hodder Children's Books
An imprint of Hachette Children's Group
Part of Hodder & Stoughton
Carmelite House
50 Victoria Embankment
London EC4Y 0DZ

A catalogue record of this book is available from the British Library.

ISBN 978 1 444 92554 8

Printed in China

An Hachette UK Company
www.hachette.co.uk

MIX
Paper from
responsible sources
FSC® C104740

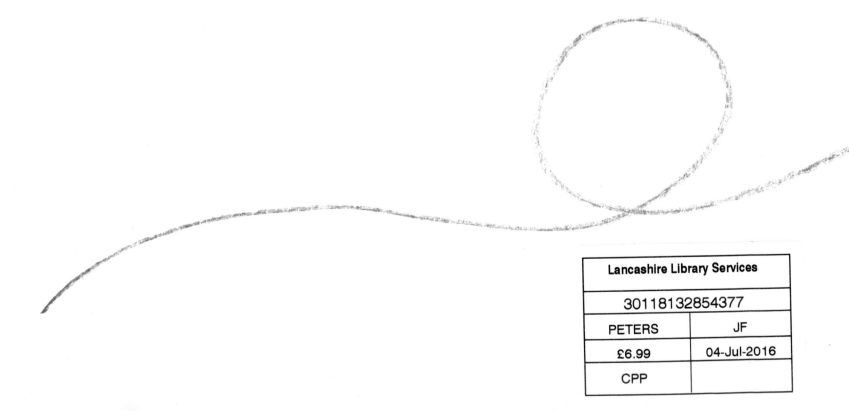

THE QUEEN'S HANDBAG

Steve Antony

Hodder
Children's
Books

The Queen was ready for her
tour of **Great Britain** when...

swoosh!

A sneaky swan swooped off with her handbag!

The swan was fast,
but so was the Queen!

She drove after it to...

Windsor Castle.

Then she rode after it to...

Stonehenge.

Then she flew after it to...

the White Cliffs of Dover.

She cycled after it to...

Oxford.

She dived after it to...

Snowdonia.

She sped after it to...

the Giant's Causeway.

She chugged after it to...

the Angel of the North.

She galloped after it to...

Edinburgh Castle,

and all the way back to...

London. But the swan was nowhere to be seen,

until the Queen spotted it in...

the London Marathon,

where she finally caught the sneaky swan at...

...the finish line!